Goldilocks and the Three Bears

Caralyn Buehner & Mark Buehner

SCHOLASTIC INC.
New York Toronto London Auckland Sydney
Mexico City New Delhi Hong Kong Buenos Aires

To Matthew

ISBN-13: 978-0-545-11896-5
ISBN-10: 0-545-11896-4

Text copyright © 2007 by Caralyn Buehner.
Pictures copyright © 2007 by Mark Buehner.
All rights reserved. Published by Scholastic Inc., 557 Broadway, New York, NY 10012, by arrangement with Dial Books for Young Readers, a division of Penguin Young Readers Group, a member of Penguin Group (USA) Inc.
SCHOLASTIC and associated logos are trademarks and/or registered trademarks of Scholastic Inc.

12 11 10 9 8 7 6   11 12 13/0

Printed in the U.S.A.   40

First Scholastic printing, October 2008

Designed by Lily Malcom

Text set in Garamond

The art was prepared by using oil paints over acrylics.

Readers, see if you can find a cat, a rabbit, and a Tyrannosaurus rex hidden in each picture.

Once upon a time, in a little house in the woods, there lived a family of bears. They were Papa Bear, Mama Bear, and Little Wee Bear.

Every morning the bear family sat down to eat breakfast, and every morning their breakfast was the same: a bowl of porridge. But one morning, no one was able to eat any porridge at all.

"This porridge is TOO HOT!" Papa Bear exclaimed, after tasting a bite from his great big bowl.

Mama Bear took a small nibble of the small bit of porridge from her medium-sized bowl. "Oh dear," she said. "It *is* too hot."

Little Wee Bear, who loved porridge more than anything, took the biggest bite he could from his little wee bowl. When Mama and Papa looked at him, he tried to say, "My porridge is JUST RIGHT," but because his mouth was so full it sounded like: "My porch has a bus light."

"Hmmmmm," said Papa Bear.

"I know what we'll do," said Mama Bear. "Let's all go for a walk. By the time we come back home, our porridge will be perfect." So Papa Bear grabbed his hat, and Mama Bear grabbed Little Wee Bear's hand. Little Wee Bear tried to grab his bowl of porridge, but Mama Bear was already out the door.

Off they lumbered down the path.

The bear family was hardly out of sight when a little girl with yellow curls came skipping rope down the path. She skipped right up to the little house, pounded on the door, and sang:

"Tra-la-la and tee-hee-hee.
Won't you come and jump with me?"

Of course, no one was home, so no one answered.

The little girl, whose name was Goldilocks, tried again. "Hey!" She banged on the door, and this time it flew open. Goldilocks skipped into the living room without missing a step. When she saw the three bears' chairs, she chanted:

"Big chair, middle chair, little chair too,
Somebody's here to *bounce* on you!"

Goldilocks pulled herself up on Papa Bear's big chair and jumped.

"This chair has no bounce at all . . . "

Next she climbed on Mama Bear's medium-sized chair, but as soon as she tried to stand up, she sank right down inside.

"This chair makes me feel so small . . . "

Then Goldilocks looked over at the little wee chair for Little Wee
Bear and grinned.

"But *that* chair looks like it's just right.
I'll jump me up an appetite!"

She climbed up on the little wee chair. She jumped, and the chair bounced.
Goldilocks jumped and bounced, jumped and bounced until she jumped right
through the seat of the little wee chair.

"Oopsy-daisy! What a mess!" She giggled. "Bounced a bit too much, I guess."
But she hopped right up when she saw the three bowls of porridge on the table
and started skipping rope again.

"Porridge, porridge, sittin' in a bowl,
I'm gonna eat until I'm full!"

Goldilocks tasted a spoonful of porridge from the great big bowl.

"OUCH!" She spit out the huge mouthful of porridge. "This porridge is too hot!"

Next Goldilocks helped herself to a spoonful of porridge from the medium-sized bowl.

She shivered. "This one certainly is not!"

Then Goldilocks tasted a spoonful of the porridge in the little wee bowl.

"Yum-yum!" she mumbled. "Finally! This porridge tastes just right to me!"

Goldilocks ate and ate until there wasn't even one bit left
in the little wee bowl. Then she let out an enormous yawn.

"Goodness, I'm a sleepyhead!
I think I'll jump right into bed!"

Goldilocks skipped up the stairs.

When she saw Papa Bear's great big bed, she climbed up and flopped back on the pillow.

Immediately she sat up, rubbing her head.

"This bed feels like a big old brick!"

She climbed onto the silky medium-sized bed that was Mama Bear's. But as soon as she lay down, she slid off the end of the bed and bounced onto the floor.

"This bed here is much too slick!"

Then Goldilocks spied Little Wee Bear's little wee bed.

"Oh, I hope with all my might that
This wee bed will be *just right* . . ."

Goldilocks tucked herself in the cozy little bed, with her jump rope curled up beside her. Soon she was sound asleep.

Meanwhile, Mama Bear, Papa Bear, and Little Wee Bear were just returning from their walk.

They were very hungry, but when they saw that the door to their house was open, they stopped.

"How very strange!" said Papa Bear.

"Do you think someone's inside?" asked Mama Bear.

"Maybe it's a wild beast!" Little Wee Bear squealed.

The bear family hurried into the living room. There was no mistake about it.
"Someone's been sitting in my chair!" exclaimed Papa Bear.

"Someone's been sitting in my chair!" cried Mama Bear.

"Look!" Little Wee Bear's eyes grew very big as he pointed to the mess on the floor. "Something's been sitting in my chair too, and broke it to bits! Maybe it was a monster!"

Then the three bears saw the table.
"SOMEONE'S BEEN EATING MY PORRIDGE!" roared Papa Bear.
"Someone's been eating *my* porridge!" wailed Mama Bear.
Little Wee Bear looked sadly at his bowl. "Something has *eaten* my porridge. I think it was an alien!"

The three bears were very disturbed. Together they tiptoed up to the bedroom.

"My bed!" Papa Bear sputtered. "Someone's been lying on my bed!"

"Look!" Mama Bear whispered. "Someone's been lying on my bed too."

"Something's been lying on my bed"—Little Wee Bear pointed to his little wee bed—"and I think it's still there!"

The three bears crept over to the little wee bed. When they saw Goldilocks, they were very frightened.

"It's a wild beast!" Papa Bear growled.

"It's a monster!" moaned Mama Bear.

"It's an alien!" Little Wee Bear whispered excitedly.

The bear family didn't know what to do. Finally Little Wee Bear reached out and poked the jump rope.

Goldilocks's eyes popped open.

"Eeeeeeek!" cried the three bears.

"Eeeeeeek!" screamed Goldilocks. Then she threw off the covers and sprang out of bed.

"Pardon me if I don't stay . . .
Don't feel like jumping anyway!"

Goldilocks leaped out of the window and ran away before the three
bears had even stopped yelling.

The bears watched until Goldilocks was out of sight.

"I declare!" Mama Bear exclaimed. "I'm so upset, I couldn't eat a bite!"
Papa Bear looked at Little Wee Bear, and Little Wee Bear looked at Papa Bear.
"*We* could," they said.
"HMMPFF!" Mama Bear rolled her eyes. But she mixed up another huge pot
of porridge anyway.

And this time it was *just right*.